Hubble

For Martin, with love

Previous publications:
Catching the Light (Slow Dancer, 1996)
The Blue Bang Theory (a collection of four poets) (Redbeck Press, 1997)

Acknowledgements
Some of the poems in this book have appeared in the following magazines: *Poetry & Audience, The Swansea Review, Poetry Life, Nova Poetica, Poetry Nottingham International, Borderlines, Staple, Organisation & Environment* (USA), *Oxford Poetry, The Frogmore Papers, The Bound Spiral, Writing Women, Poetry Wales, The Rialto, Ambit* and *Poetry Ireland Review*; and in the anthology *Stone Circle* (Blue Nose Poets).

Hubble

Diana Syder

Smith/Doorstop Books

Published 1997 by
Smith/Doorstop Books
The Poetry Business
The Studio
Byram Arcade
Westgate
Huddersfield HD1 1ND

ISBN 1 869961 84 6

British Library Cataloguing-in-Publication Data. A catalogue record for this book is available from the British Library.

Typeset at The Poetry Business
Printed by Peepal Tree Press, Leeds

Distributed by Password (Books) Ltd.,
23 New Mount Street, Manchester M4 4DE

Cover by blue door design, Heckmondwike
Cover image is by courtesy of NASA, from a detail of the Cartwheel Galaxy, taken by the Hubble Space Telescope Wide Field Planetary Camera 2.

The Poetry Business acknowledges the help of Kirklees Metropolitan Council and Yorkshire & Humberside Arts.

CONTENTS

III *Waves*

I

Hubble

Hubble

It doesn't look much, swathed in tin foil, its solar panels
all but juddering themselves to bits sixteen times a day

every time it passes from day to night, big as a Sheffield bus
shining in starlight and doing 500 mph over Madagascar.

And it wasn't easy getting it up here, all that hellfire steam
and thundering flame at Cape Canaveral to kick the earth away,

hardly subtle, hardly how you'd choose to get a piece
of precision engineering where you want it and hit

the exact place where the lures of space counteract
the attractions of earth, but here it is and it works, so I take

my hat off to the bright spark who dreamed it right at the start
and take it off again to what's in us that wants to unzip

everything right up to the edge of time and only stop then
because we'll have to, but at least to get that far and see.

The photos are out of this world. Look at this one: a jet of gas
from a young star in Orion and it has it perfectly, just as it is,

or was, because we're travelling in time by standing still,
seeing out and way back to whatever made us. If angels

do anything like this then sign me up because I'm a believer.
OK, an arms akimbo, mock-up angel, with bits sticking out

all over the place that would have no grace on earth
but I can extrapolate and this is all about imagination, in fact

I have to remind myself these are pictures of real things:
whole cities of stars, brown dwarfs, blue stragglers, plus exotics

I've never heard of. Eleven billion years for the universe
to invent a way of looking at itself and I'm around to see it!

I could look for a lifetime and probably will. I'd love to tell them,
Galileo, Bruno and the others, right up to Hubble himself,

see what they all made of it – or would that not be fair?
Might it be too much to bear, your own beliefs coming true

because what price dreams then? Anyway, talking of interactions
between people and light makes it sound more grandiose

than it really is, when what goes on most days is stumbling around
heavy as lead, trying to find a good way of living and mostly

I'm tied up with that, but I sometimes get hit by something coming
out of the ether at me, like the phrase *tomorrow is a new day*,

just as I heard it drop ready formed into my mind as a consequence
of nothing related and took note because it sounded hopeful

and made me think of all the new days as they regularly fall,
the shadow backing off from the Pacific, America, the Atlantic.

All the people waking, yawning and sitting up, one group
after another as the light approaches, doing it in reverse

when night returns, oscillating between gravity, which could pin
us to the ground and imagination, which might spin us away –

and here's a platform for imagination if ever there was one!
It'll keep us busy for ages, working out how much is true

and how much more there is of what we need to know
to swim strong and well in our deep mysterious bell,

with bubbles rising slowly out of the past, present and future
and some of the dreams coming true for us, one secret at a time.

Eye Test

Keep looking
she says, shining the light straight in.
Now look right. Look left.
What materialises is a pinkish sheet
with little red snakes swimming so clear
I can focus on the ends of them,
how they taper in mid air.

I know what it is instantly
but can't work out how
it would happen like that,
me seeing my own retina,
the clever darling of it.

Look right again. Left.
This time it's harder with the red
snakes demanding attention.
I want to fix them in my mind's eye
and try to remember what I once knew
about rods and cones and eight neural layers –
or was it five? – a vertical arrangement of cells
at any rate with the second cranial nerve leading
away and something remote about receptor
mechanisms and sensitivity, the vast speed.

Now read the bottom line.
Everything seems normal.
But it isn't, not with this red
and orange excitement, this flush
of tenderness for the layer of mucosa
at the back of my eye, the way it works,
being in love at first sight.

Costar. Before and After

*In 1993 NASA sent up seven astronauts to instal COSTAR,
a black box that would counteract the fault in Hubble's
mirror, as described and illustrated in* A Journey Through
Time, *Barbree & Caidin*

You wouldn't think it would matter –
out by 10 thousandths of an inch or 1/50th
the diameter of a human hair, the mirror
ending up 2 millionths of a metre too flat
but at distances like these it doesn't take much,

like the way it shows star Melnick 34
in the Large Magellanic Cloud as a blur
on page 21, a creamy centre flowing wet
on wet and curdling into filmy space,
awe-inspiring though, like vague things can be.

On page 22 you can't believe your eyes
how distinct Melnick is, a spiral of violet
and burnt orange, phosphorus and rose,
with sparks spinning off the edge like it might
start to slowly waltz round any minute.

The colours have a shine to them
even on paper and with a deep vision reach
of 12 billion miles there's an illusion
of intimacy, ah, that Melnick, good old
Melnick, but I still can't sort out scale

and keep reminding myself just what
these pictures are of because it doesn't
come naturally, what I tend to do is scale them
down to meet me till it's no big deal to hide
a galaxy with a finger tip. Strange,

the size we think we are when there's
such clear cut evidence to the contrary.
Anyone can see the universe going about
the vast business of expressing itself,
all we have to do is open a book.

Prayer to a Telescope

Let me always want to see beyond the edge of things even if
the means hasn't been invented and my understanding
leaves a lot to be desired.

Let me grasp just enough of optics to love the laws of light
and be grateful for eyes, especially mine.

Let me appreciate coloured photos – the airglow above the
earth's horizon, I'll never forget that – but let me relate to
black and white things also; coffee, a cup, a magpie against
the snow and jasmine indoors in January.

Let me love the leaden shadows and tune in to the spectrum
that permeates the night.

Let me keep an open mind and stay up to date so I under-
stand as much as I can in the time I've got and not, in my
lifetime, reach the limits of my imagination.

Let me balance everything and find a way to handle scale that
stops me dwindling in the presence of large numbers, but
rather keeps me lifesize, offering what I can.

The Water Planet

I go down into the earth on an escalator through
a rocky tunnel where the sweat of living things condenses

and sometimes this part is quick, straight down
to a warm cave where there's a green-tiled pool.

All the creeping water seeps through cracks and gathers
here but I've made the pool very clear and well lit

from below with light rippling over the walls
so I can slip easily into the warm green water.

If I want to go deeper I know exactly where to dive
to find the tunnel that is short enough to do on one breath

and comes out through an opening in the giant cliff face
which is the underneath rim of the earth's great curve.

I hang in infinite depth, breathing easily because this
is the well of the earth in which all things first belong

but I daren't go far, it's too cloudy with minerals and solutes
so a few strokes in a circle and my mind's eye pans back

till my body's a speck and there's warmth, a steep sense
of the vertical and of the interior. If I let my body shrink

further there'd be cliff and water without me, but I don't
like the risk of it and zoom back to where I'm life size.

I never stay long, because this is the source
of the world in which all things finally dissolve.

The 'L' Word

1. Master Race

It will be the cockroaches who go about their business
as if nothing had changed, on the day after that day
when the last wisps of the ozone finally disperse.
We might consider their single-minded absorption
in their own affairs distasteful, if we were around to,
and it certainly turns upside down everything I was taught
about the food pyramid, whoever arranged it like that,
like a mountain, something to be climbed and sat on,
has a lot to answer for – if all the time it's been a valley
with insects swarming in the sky at the top.

2. The Lab Technician's Monday Morning

*When the Apollo 12 crew returned from the moon they brought
with them fragments of the wrecked Surveyor 3. These were later
found to harbour bacteria, Streptococcus mitis.*

I'm watching them grow against the odds
and culturing them according to instructions.
I didn't think they would and then this morning ...
        one patch spreading into another.

You'd never expect them to survive lift-off, the trip,
two years in the desiccated vacuum of the moon,
extremes of heat and cold, shrivelling radiation,
        then getting themselves back

and I reckon there's something about a creature
that can wait it out on the off chance, slow everything down
to just this side of stop and preserve an inclination to divide
        through all that.

So maybe he's right, the guy who says
we came here on meteorites from somewhere else.
In my book, you keep an eye on a life form
        as cunning as that.

3. Europa

Any old astrobiologist will tell you
that a quarter by weight of all the life
on earth is made up of ants, yet from five feet
off the ground we hardly see them
and from 600 miles up, there's not a trace
of life on earth, only water gives us away.

So when he looks at Europa's icy surface,
an ocean frozen 60 miles deep, it's the best bet
for the 'L' word in our solar system, because things
can survive winter at the bottom of a lake.
Which is why he scans what's out there
for some watery world near a moderate star.

And what he can't understand is why the rest
of us carry on as if it's all science fiction,
when so many suns are up there, the odds
are a trillion to one against *not* finding something.
Odd that when it happens it'll come
as a shock, even to him. Any day now.

The Astronaut Drifts

It was bad when the figures went inside and again
when you couldn't make the module out at all.
When you said goodbye to your wife and friends
it was a ragged ending like waiting till a train leaves
and you were sweating but your feet were cold.

Your life floated around you, the bad bits taking longer
to disperse and then came random as photons
against your suit so Control offered you counselling
or a cleric of your choice but you asked for music,
Pachelbel's Canon, because you heard it once
with black balloons cruising across the sky, each one
carrying a flare and the whole thing was exquisite.
You'd like to go as a son et lumière but what you got
was easy listening which you turned off. Silence.

How long? One day? two? three? Any time now you'll need a pee
and your feet are bloody freezing. If you're going to die
you may as well make the most of it. Fly. Try for somersaults
or – go on, no one's looking – pretend it's yours, that you made
the whole damn thing. What about swimming naked
in a glorious surrender ... even ... if you took the helmet off ...
would there be time to see what nothing smells like?

That would get it over with and what a way to go,
your sucked out molecules shifting back and forth
between the interstellar spaces, who knows, they might
beach one day on some bare rock in a backwater
of the universe and kick start the whole thing over.
Would that be enough for you?

Classified

DON'T MISS the ultimate one way trip! Launch takes place
just before death in a pressurised, see-through shroud.
This is common practice and there is no pain, instead a feeling
of WELL BEING while listening to your favourite music
on handcrafted speakers. We have an EXTENSIVE RANGE
of Requiems and Fanfares – our trained experts are happy to advise.

If you opt for a multiple launch, our SPECIAL OFFER at half
the price is based on two or more sharing – imagine dandelion
seeds drifting out at random – either way, with the suit
programmed to self-destruct in 24 hours, after seeing it close to,
you really do become one with the Cosmos. Remember,
BOOK EARLY to avoid disappointment.

Space travel's old hat, the safe dispersal of organic stuff
is what matters so put your molecules back where they belong
and for those of you for whom this feels bleak, pay that little
bit extra and have the Walkman survive for another week,
playing a compilation from the constellation of your choice.
Don't delay. Send for your FREE COLOUR BROCHURE today.

Hyakutake

The Independent expects a once-in-a-lifetime miracle as the comet skims far closer to the earth than any other heavenly body. It plots Hyakutake's position on selected days:

1 April: Venus at greatest eastern elongation
Venus dazzling. Magical. My brother phoning to say he'd be failing in his duty as Family Astronomer if he didn't tell us to get outside and look near the Pole Star oh and by the way, his team have found three more carbon bodies on the edge of the universe, definite this time, in fact three of the ten oldest objects in the known universe, he thought he'd just mention it.

3 April: beginning of total eclipse of the moon
Driving up to the Edge to get above the valley lights. Laughter lower down and *Kumbayah* from rocks further up. Moon full and smouldering. Lying back on the bonnet there's no Milky Way and no comet either. We make excuses for it. The charred moon's swinging about like a mad thing inside the binoculars then I have it, whatever sea I'm looking at puckers. The car won't start. Nine tries then still something odd about the lights so coming down on nothing or full beam.

4 April: end of eclipse
I'm tuned in and not wanting to tune out, but having to drive to work. On Houndkirk Moor there's a man astride the ridge tiles on the roof of Fox House, and I only just spot him because he's the colour of stone himself, but he can see for miles, the first sunny day after a long winter and all the distances graphite blue, which means any minute the mist could come back down.

11 April: moon at last quarter
Driving out of Keighley towards a sky the colour of an unlit candle, I tell Sara that right now Hubble can see so far out it reaches 60 per cent of the way back into all the past there is, and before it's finished it'll reach back 90, which is nothing compared to the next generation of instruments because they'll go all the way and photograph the Creation. She says, what a thought, that it's all she can do to think about it and keep the car on the road.

17 April: new moon
Mother phones to complain about now as usual and to talk
about the past, which never sounds rosy but it's where her
heart is. The future's a malevolent thing we're all forced into,
which at her age wouldn't be unusual but for someone who
claims the gift of prophecy she's spent a hell of a lot of time
looking the other way. Scrap nostalgia, I say, give me 21st
Century dental care any day.

21 April: maximum of Lyrid meteors
Got it! Directly over the pub. A smear of light. Trying to think
of tons of rock and ice and failing. The Milky Way was an
animal's backbone that stopped the sky crashing down in
pieces, or it was drops of milk spilt from Hera's breasts. Not
long ago I'd have been glad to know but stories aren't big
enough, not even for the inkling I have of what's out there.
The more I grasp how vast everything is, how small we are,
the more puzzled I am that we have any foothold at all …
What to make of it.

23 April: Mercury at greatest eastern elongation
Lu Bin and Shaomei's firstborn is Year of the Rat. Asked Lu
Bin if newborns can see their own fingers. When the baby
moves her finger tip to touch her nose, that finger comes
nearer to the present, because light travels less distance to
reach her eyes, infinitesimally, but the principle is there, from
which it follows that, in theory, Jessica Wang's fingers are
older than her toes. She knows.

25 April: moon at first quarter
It's gone. On our flat roof and looking up I run out of zeros. A
speckled mixture of all the times at once is gathered in my
present. A feeling agitates my diaphragm, works its way up. If
it had a voice that feeling would be saying *Go on, go on! Run
and run and run for the arc of the future. Do your very best
with it.*

II

The Tuna is an Interesting Fish

1.

In the beginning:
that index finger, the spark leaping outwards.
Then blue-white stars on the edge of the great spirals,
the planet turning heavy elements at its core.
A film of water. Lightning and the first replicating molecules.
A seed. A soft felt over the surface.

2.

A man is on his knees examining a patch of grass,
describing its genes, its chemistry, its multiple physiologies.
It'll take him a life-time but who wouldn't give a lifetime
any day, he says, to know the meaning of grass?
It could be worse, he adds, if he'd chosen instead
a deep sea fish that he couldn't see with his own eyes
or smell, or touch, he'd never get the full picture.

So he's done a painting of stalks, tasted some,
written a poem, a tune, blown raspberries
in his hands across a blade of it. The painting
does not smell of green, the smell is in that bottle
and he's working on it, says the main thing is not
to look up, because there'd be the shock of more
and what on earth would he do with a planetful?

3.

Meanwhile, the tuna is an interesting fish.
It turns thermodynamics upside down
by accelerating faster and leaping higher
than it ought to be able to, which sets
a precedent for human thought.

So someone built a model in a tank at M.I.T.
and found that what the clever tuna does
is to swim in circles, churning up a vortex
from which it launches and rockets away.

4.

It can drive you crazy wondering why
the grass bothers, and what the tuna makes
of it all, so one friend wants to know what's wrong
with having a box marked 'Mystery' and enjoying
not knowing, which is new to me and sounds
a great way of having a rest from First Causes,
final theories and my own behaviour.

Having said that, who'd have predicted
the detail of grass when we first set out?
Besides, when I see lightning charge the earth
with eighty thousand volts of sky and know
I know there's lightning on Jupiter, I'm glad.
And snow on the TV being radiation left over
from the Big Bang – I'm glad I know that too.

5.

We are all in a restaurant by the sea,
lots of nets and floats and illuminated fish tanks
with waves just over the wall and I love it, being so close.

It has to be mullet I say, my mouth watering
and tell myself that the one in the tank
looking straight at me couldn't possibly know
or remember and that the irony of the swell
only a few feet away is wasted on it
but can we ever be certain ...

and in that hesitation I am become Fish,
my face pressed to the edge of the glass
all eyes and mouth, straining to sort my own reflection
from what's out there but then the food arrives

and I'm not Fish, I'm eating it, with an inkling
of how breath-taking that would be –
the fish's first realisation of water.

Copernicus Explains Himself to God

I am afraid of the silly clergy,
their grim pursuit of the human soul, the Holy Writ
that puts Man at the centre, the special child.
I have reasoned it is not like this
and have condemned myself. So it must wait.

Lord, upon my death
I will give them the calculus that parts your hand
from the hand of man. It will be my epitaph –
De Revolutionibus Orbium Coelestium –
in which Ptolemy's geocentric universe
is cast down after a thousand years
and we are made planet to a minor star

but I will stress hypothesis, it will be hypothesis only.
Lord, forgive both my arrogance and cowardice.
The clue is Ptolemy's equant, which just offsets
the centre of motion from the centre of the Earth
and shows how you have commanded the Lantern
of the universe, the most beautiful Temple
to stand still and not the Earth.

Old fool they will say, the biblemongers,
*his mind plays tricks, this motion would shake the earth to bits
and gales and storms would overcome us all.*
I cannot answer this.

And my soul?
It is both comfort and torment not to see beyond my death.
Yet I am curious. Aye. And afraid to die not knowing
which of my work lives on, in what regard,
or what solutions future years might yield.

Blessed are those who will know, with casual interest,
the outcome. In Hell I'll never see the great orbs,
the truth of their scriven circles and whether men
on Earth speak well or ill of me or not at all.

Galileo Talks to Copernicus.
And I Have a Word with the Pope.

I saw for the first time the mountains of the moon
with their great shadows, the Milky Way as separate stars,
sunspots, Venus' phases, the strange nature of Saturn.
Most wonderful of all – Jupiter with his four satellite moons.

At last, our argument against the pious men
who thought that if the Earth moved round the sun
we'd leave the moon behind. Not so. If Jupiter
can carry four, why not Earth a single sphere?

The Jesuits refused to look through,
said I worked against the Scriptures. Unjust. Untrue.
I marvel at God's work and because I do I grieve
for your sublime intellect, your outlawed soul.

How dare those dull, dim-witted men
meddle with God's revelations. They still do –
my ill-fated *Dialogue*. It was folly to publish
before my death. Would that I had learned from you.

Recant or death. The Inquisition had me choose.
The trial was cruel and no less cruel the last nine years
a prisoner. My own house. How everything circles.
They were indulgent. Poor Bruno went to the stake.

Praise God I have my telescope. It multiplies the heavens
by thirty fold and though I cannot undo these walls
nor walk into the view, by night I roam among the stars.
Their witness is glorious and cold. I grow old here.

> *In 1992 the Vatican published 'Studi Galieani', the result of an*
> *eleven year impartial consideration of the case by a Papal*
> *Commission. After this, Pope John Paul II made an official*
> *apology.*

Who to?
Say it, John Paul, to the mountains of the moon,
say it out loud to the sun, the receding galaxies,

kneel on your small balcony before Jupiter
and make your sounds at the wild sky. Convince the earth.
Say it night after travelling night as you grow old,
deliver it, trembling, on your final breath.

Notre Dame

Illumination soaks the floor, is smudged in by treading feet.
I think of the optics; filters, angles, coloured light,
then $E=mc^2$ where c is the velocity of light,
m is mass and E, all the Energy in the universe
which is constant. I regret God, who was easy.

We have built what we wanted.
I can see the shape of it, it is big as a cathedral.
The dimensions of absence are a vacuum I rush to fill –
what this cathedral lacks is a tree because nothing
lives in here except all of us trundling through.

Right now I can get no further than how leaves might look
against the dark. I light a ten franc candle at the feet
of Jeanne d'Arc, weigh her conviction against my lack.
It's a knack to balance the little flame that fills a certain gap.
It will burn for an hour in as good a place as any.

CERN

In theory it should get easier as we go on,
this drive to fundamentals, but believing
isn't the same as understanding and being in two places at once
isn't part of our everyday language – as if a speck of light
can choose to be where or when in the universe
or an uncertain cat could make up its mind.

As though time itself could begin at the Big Bang
and not a moment before except – this is one idea –
fields of potentiality, fluctuations in the vacuum
plus whatever caused those fields to exist. These are less
than miniature problems, we're down to the nature
of nothing, which adds up but doesn't make sense.

In any case why simplify? Diversity
takes my breath away, our countless identities
crowding every split second. Where on earth to start?
Try Fly Agaric, Heath Bedstraw, the 300 ft long
blades of sea plants, early gorse, seeds,
you and I being different. And profligacy:

take a bracket fungus smoking millions of spores.
Take 13,000 lichens, 1,000 species of mistletoe
and what we know about sperm, March and our swifts
fetching and carrying till the cat hooked one
with a definite paw, or take an oak heaving tons of water
up its trunk everyday and losing most of it.

Following the moods of even one cell is like trying to guess
the mind of an animal that keeps on building,
unable to stop dismantling and reassembling the particles
of each day as if all that mattered was to carry on
doing this, maintaining the massive circle,
the high-energy transformation of light.

CERN: the particle accelerator, Geneva

29

The Origin of Zero

Nothing is a wild beast roaming the universe,
pacing the unthinkable edge, before time, before space.
Nothing ever, an unresounding gap that won't hold still.

The Chinese invented what they couldn't imagine,
first left the space on the counting board, understood
that how we write a number is important, with their black
and red beads, odds and evens, lucky, unlucky numbers:
1 cow   no cows
10 bowls   no bowls
100 grains of rice   no grains of rice.

Something about events in AD 683 laid down
for the first time a written sign for the absence of number,
Cambodia and Sumatra figuring it out simultaneously.
Not surprising, with the Hindu 'void' on one side,
Taoist 'emptiness' the other. When there's nothing in front
and at your back, you need a fixed point more than anything.

Anything doesn't need a number but *nothing* is impossible.
So we enclose, with our lips, the sound ... O,
capture with our pens the empty space, the written nought
as if we thought it was that simple to stop emptiness
clamouring through the limits of our imagination.

The Blue Bang Theory

We hit upon it
in the sort of conversation you have
with an astrophysicist
after several glasses of wine
at that sort of post-christening buffet

that In the Beginning
was an infinite number
of delphiniums, infinitely blue,
cramped into an infinitesimal space
and that before this, there was nothing
in the way of delphiniums
we can ever know about.

Unstable, that concentration of buds.
Something had to give or happen. It did.

It must have been absolutely glorious.
A billion summers all going off at once,
after which the sky settled down
to a steady background flowering.

And so pleased with ourselves
we called for a piece of the cake
and more wine please
and debated the existence
of anti-delphiniums somewhere.

All afternoon the baby's spacious eyes
were entirely open-minded.

Judge Davies Does the Ironing

And he's just ironed a spider, steamed it flat,
a short hiss marking the end of it.
He's apologised to God, whom he doesn't believe in,
for his small sin but wonders if it *is* small or whether
it counts at all seeing as it was accidental.

Now it's a Rorschach spider. He stares
at what he's done, the inkblot shape essentially octagonal,
and is suddenly aware of all the other spiders, their grief
crescendos in the walls and floors and beyond that,
crowds of flies are cheering.

He gets a grip. Only he and the spider know
and the spider couldn't have had a grasp of it
which leaves him sole witness. And perhaps God,
(in whom he doesn't believe). Does a spider matter?
He can't decide, even a small death is not simple.

But it is. A tiny fizz. As simple as that.

The Squeamish Nature Lover

Three things I want to do before I die:

1. Swim naked in the sea, unashamed,
   touching everything at once.
2. Embrace my lawn in the rain, prostrate
   at night beneath the wide open beech.
3. Touch an earthworm or a slug.

But I couldn't ever, that last one. No Way.
Why not? I wish I knew. If I were a naturalist –
that practical way they have of laying something out
on their palm, nudging it with an index finger.
Or how they plunge their bare arms
right up to the elbows in leaf mould, slime trails
and fungal threads, oblivious to the eggs of monsters.

My small mind oozes its anaerobic nightmare
of mucus, tissue, the noxious details of living slop.
My love is skin-deep, satisfied with the documentary,
the view from the car and I'm scared
to face the soil, to lie on it naked.

So if I want to rescue an earthworm or a slug
I must approach well-armed with stones and sticks
with which to flick the thing to safety and apologise
for probably doing more harm than good.

This is not enough. Beware, all stranded worms and slugs.
My love is partial, afraid of your slippery night,
your fronds, your ivy trails. Don't reason with me.

I cannot move my finger closer.

Bracken

Two fronds turning early,
freak coral spikes
against all the green.

What gene describes this,
that these two should stand out
as if some arsonist

had thrown a match
and started slick botanical
tongues of flame

and sent a million spores
smoking through
the carcinogenic hedgerow?

It doesn't surprise me
about bracken – the chill
September always did have

if you breathed deep enough …
or when you were coming
off the moor through shoulder-deep,

vegetable seas,
even then, something
underneath, biding its time.

A Limestone House

280 million years ago this heap of stones
was a fluid acre of thin-shelled corals.
Forests of stone lilies were bending
and unbending in local tides that ran

along the shallow, sunlit floor
and bubbles flared and spent themselves
over feather-boned crinoids and trilobites.
Shells and parts of shells drizzled down, crushing

and being crushed, squeezing the light out
and then darkness itself compressed, aeons of it,
until the sound of men and the hammer-bright
light of day again on primitive surfaces,

brilliant and dissolving in the long-lived rain.
Our once swimming house has settled
rock-solid around us and this far from a sea
the stone is still, except sometimes at night

when things tick on and off and come again
and then for no good reason I wake
to what could be a sense of floating, a love
of salts, an understanding of gravity.

Making it Up

A big woman in ordinary clothes
was bending towards an easel of birch twigs.
All around was snow, but in the clearing
each brown dry sound was of beech mast,
birds perhaps. This was very clear. As was her voice.

Don't steal my milk, she said without turning round.
And she never slowed as she padded, twisted,
wrapped. The more I looked the more I saw –
the whole wild world was in there: cuckoo pint,
a mouse's foot, moleskin, a mountain, heavy rain.

Despite the snow her sculpture was of living things.
So where did the sprouting grass, the roses come from?
She fitted in a sprocket, analgesics, one diamond ring.
More: a computer, half an abbey, clingfilm,
a cloud chamber, a road, a dinosaur.

Never once did she stop to consider
where this piece might be placed or that,
as if she knew. I didn't say a thing, turned away,
convinced she would go on constructing,
fitting it all in, whatever came.

The River

There's not much sky,
just what the leaves allow.
A coot sips at margins
where the green of water transmutes,
not quite, to the green of land.
A duck sleeps out there. Drifts.

I once met the husband
of someone who drowned here.
And now something living has lifted,
so when I twist round there's only interference
patterns on water. And it's there again.

Something else complains behind the willows,
rattles its throat, settles the better for it.
Nearby there's waist-high balsam,
spent foxgloves, albino ferns. It's cumulative.
I might fall apart if anything moves
and to glance over my shoulder
could be to see everything.

In the pure time of the midstream
there's nothing happening except the duck .
It's an ugly pool for swimming,
but could, in some imagined evening light,
be so glossy dark you might wish
you were brave enough to go in at last,
to go right down into the river naked
and see how it lives.

Happy 42

Take a glass of water. Go down to the sea.
Empty the glass into the sea and allow enough years
for the water to disperse through all the oceans.
Then go back to the shore and fill your glass from the sea.

Some of the original water will be in the glass,
meaning: there are more molecules in a glass of water
than there are glasses of water in the sea.

There are parts of the ocean I can never return to,
it's easier to move on than revisit a glamorous country
where the world came out for the first time.

And I couldn't live all my life in the same place,
shedding my younger selves till the air grows thick
with their greetings and reminders.

As for Reunions, mixing our pasts and presents
with too much water and not enough bridges –
we have become stories for each other.

Yet I like being halfway through, seeing a line
to this point I didn't notice earlier on, so that
where am I going is now where have I come from.

If 'time is in the instant', what we know of time
is the evidence of it in any one shot. Freeze frame – NOW.
What I can see: crumpled clothes, split beams, dust.

These details are what I can know of time, anything more fluid
is impression. Snapshot or flow? I only know there is an ocean
in this house, that I am dispersing. So whatever anyone
wants of me, come on in and fill a glass. Fill it quickly.

An English Polka

He's one eighth Irish
and picks up the whistle to learn something new
from *1001 Irish Tunes* but today not one of them
takes his fancy enough to learn it which is unusual.

The rest is English
but he hasn't a clue how an English polka might go
or how he'd play it, in what time or key? Where he'd put
the dotted notes, what sort of ornaments or harmony.

When he was away
he wondered how our language sounds if you are Dutch or African
and kept trying until he'd an outsider's ear. It was something like
the sea falling away from shingle, both soft and hard.

And every time he's away
he considers how light hangs as he's driving home from work
to the valley which is a promised land he can sleep in,
though he's not sure if it's birthrights or just the place

your heart beats to.
He's always said the universal is what's important,
that no one can claim a particular tune unless they wrote it,
that he's a musician first, anything else comes after.

He's let his music drift,
has never needed it to stay alive but now his fingers itch.
How *might* an English polka go? The music matters,
footsteps across the shingle after dark.

Walkman

                I love
the way it tucks into my palm,
the glossy tape, the spool's perfect teeth,
the obedience of buttons.

I'm not sure what it does
                but I like having
the Dolby noise reduction system, with extra bass,
the adjustments at 330Hz , 1 and 10 kHz

                and it's amazing
how a twitch of my finger
makes things happen in a microchip
at a level I can't think down to.

                I really enjoy
being able to carry it with me,
a phase-amplifier of moods on moorland strides
or plain over-the-top orchestration for a sunset

                … yes, I adore
the music pouring straight into the middle
of my head, sluicing round meninges
and ventricles, or as if someone had stuck electrodes
right in and tickled them, causing scraps of ideas
to wriggle outwards, the excitation cascading
across synapses and the whole thing generating
a larger than life reflection that shimmers
and shifts across the sea-cave roof of my skull.

The Attraction of Mountains

The Astronomer Royal travelled north to play
a hunch (a hunch being something you're drawn to),
and camping on the lower slopes found, as he'd thought,
that the plumbline was distorted by the mountain.

From this he could work out the entire mass
of the solar system and threw a party on the strength of it
right there on the mountainside, for the cooks
and surveyors, the woman who collected kindling.

Triangulation is a way of getting your bearings,
plotting the lines that connect us to everything else
and although I know nothing about the stresses
and strains of being a mountain I do know

they can afford to take their time, while I must hurry
if I want to get things done. I know for each of us,
gravity is what it comes down to, the ground pushing
up against us, the tiny difference in my height

between morning and night and how age
squashes us gradually nearer the earth.
The past is slippery but can be ignored or at least
grown out of, the future's what we can't escape from,

a massive constant that can't be outrun, what we attract to us –
the Astronomer Royal out there on the mountainside
in the 17thC, middle of winter, with his lead weight,
pulling the mountain slowly towards him.

Everest, from Nagarkot

A low-energy ray
slit the horizon,
seventy miles away,
before the sun itself burst
the skin of the mountain.

And behind me, the shrunken moon,
the full moon that spilled over
half the sky twelve hours before,
was evaporating into the long
blue hours of the plain,

so that from my hill,
whichever way I turned
was either moon or sun
and a misty swell of mountains
rolled and lifted and fell

while the centre of gravity
of the whole earth
played about my feet
and all the coloured nights
and mornings circled about me,

who was the point of it,
about which everything spiralled;
the great and small rocks of the universe,
the gas clouds, the interstellar winds
and fuzzy galaxies.

The whole creaking orrery
of time and matter and space
was gathered to that place
just as I was lucky enough
to be standing on it.

Figures on a Hill

musician

the hill is a slow tune played on a low whistle
that is known in the creep of marrow through
the canals of every bone. It oozes from finger tips,
pours out onto the flat land and raises itself up
from the very centre. Play it all night.

mathematician

the curve as an expression of delight. Reduction
to the purest form. Hill deduced back to air, the possibilities
flowing on from one line to the next and getting down
to what's left, a harmonious transcription of relationships
in which all hills are equal and all hills are a passionate equation.

molecular biologist

a way of slipping into the nooks and crannies, seeing the oscillation
of proteins, the fickle pairings of the great DNA spirals.
It's a hectic equilibrium, an infinite pointillism in which the earth
should shake itself to bits but doesn't seem to. Time and again,
this means coming back to a hill that is not at all what it seems.

mountaineer

easy. A brisk walk at early light and safe as houses. Deciding
what to do and doing it. Solid ground. Trivial things falling away
like ice breaking, tinkling back into silence and a sense
of how the hill roots itself. From this height, it's safe to scan
the earth for bigger things. The climbs of life *are* its meaning.

astrologer

gather it all in from here, destiny, scoop it out the sky
by the handful, all the migrating crabs and bulls.
A house. Build a house here and lie on the roof
listening to music and bathe in the auspicious air
and then come in waving little diagrams like star flowers.

astronomer

this far from a city the sky is properly dark and it seems
everything can be worked out from a platform like this,
where flesh is thin air for radiation to rinse through
and imagination goes 3D in the echoing spaces.
Given a high place, it's easy to think big.

linguist

when it slides out over a humped tongue
the formants of the vowel are weather, the aspirate
is an acoustic bird and voicing is heavy soil in the silences.
thebirdisflyingoverthehill. Hill. Only by naming
does it separate from its surroundings.

poet

at worst a cliche to keep slipping into, at best a metaphor
that gives meaning to something which, by itself, isn't enough.
The bottom line is whether a poem comes out of it, in fact
the more intensely the hill is itself, the more essential the poem is.
Odd that, but a great comfort, the bottom line.

The Naming of Neptune

for Mick and Sara

Why Neptune? In what way was it fluid, this speck
in the sky and what alternatives were there? Strange

how Neptune suits it, that it does have oceanic qualities
and now nothing else would do, as if we crave

our gods, our magic, after all. But I've never
seen it and probably never will, so the only difference

is that now there's a neural pathway and Neptune
has an atmosphere in the deep space of my head.

Dissection

'It's flaky'
explains my post-grad,
'gets in your nails
and you can just about forget
what you're dealing with
till you see the hairs,
then you remember.

In their earlobes, nostrils,
on their chins as well.
Honest to God, hairs!

And it's when he pulls back
skin from a cheek
and says "Here, this face
is better than that one"

and he holds it up,
offers it, drips brain juice
on our books.'

She mock retches,
swigs her Guinness.

'And then we go out
and can't eat tuna
and cottage cheese
is something else.'

The Dissection Room

Could I leave my body to science,
give up any idea of becoming a tree?
If so, what youngsters would discuss
their lovers across me? Who'd pull a face
at the slip on the knife, that first cut?

You took me round once, made jokes
about a skeleton staff, how it was all quite 'armless.
And none of the sheets covered the full length,
so the crowns of their heads, the soles
of their feet showed through.

And someone asked how
I could bare to be touched by you.

                    *

Smooth and lovely is my skin, you tell me this.
The proportions, curves, planes, you've seen before
all shapes and sizes, there's nothing you haven't seen,
so all the more surprising how you're taken

by my nakedness around the house,
how you're pleased by my torso in the bath
or sleeping or dressing – this relaxed approach
just isn't what you've had before.

We both talk technicalities, submitting layer by layer
as if we each could really know the inside of the other
and I want to indulge the simple chemical greed
of my need to talk to you in warm shapes;

this is the hind-brain, my darling,
this the curly cerebellum and here
the breast, the heart. Lower down
the rushing of my thighs is firelight

and the great frontier of my skin glows.
Your hands make rabbit shadows. Mine too,
playing games with our bodies
till it's late and the room goes cold.

The Russian Experiment

We volunteered.
All of us who had a love of aviation, who loved the sky
or dreamed of being allowed to fly, we put our passion
into getting others there, glad to be part.

They showed us a film
of the animals who went before. A weightless bird
rolled upside down, fluttering its wings
and banging into things over and over.

I remember everything.
Being suspended on a trolley when the anaesthetic
went in, cold surging up from my feet to meet the rest of me
dissolving in flaming colours from the head down.

I do not know what they gave me
but it destroyed all pain. Released from flesh
and chemistry I was remote from the earth's problems.
Fear departed like an old dog and I was floating.

Four times I went unconscious.
Each time I revived they gave me more
and coming back was harder, who would want to?
I went beyond God who cannot compare.

Nothing since has been the same.
My veins ache, my brain searches its circuits for a clue,
swings around and around but stays tied down
to blood and bone and I cannot get back.

I could not have foreseen
wanting more and more of it. Nothing can ever come again
to me that measures near to that, not even death.
This is my bundle of sorrow. It does not keep me warm.

Jacob's Ladder

1.   What's important, if you live in Madagascar,
is turning the ancestors, building them a tomb
that would do a king proud because life is short
and death is forever, taking the bones in procession
round the village, bringing the dead up to date
and when it's been done and everyone's gone home,
leaving the dead to their clean linen. Stillness.

A bird of paradise flits past. Other birds sing
for pleasure across the rice fields in the evening sun
and there's a water snake or a snake in the grass,
a flaw perhaps, that which gives us love
but then the knowledge of it, then gives us
grief and the knowledge of that too.

When the snake has its fangs in a terrified man,
what use is his consciousness then, and those
who see it happen, how not to take sides?
To transcend our panic at a moment like that,
or to step beyond ourselves at any moment,
now that would be something,

but when my own Armageddon pillows up,
a wall of black smoke across the field,
I still end up begging something to give way
or that some ancestor might intercede,
just a trace of it, barely detectable
but it annoys me, that last minute gap
between what I believe, what I can't do without.

2.   They have almost explained music.
It is wonderful, the right brain putting in the emotion,
what the technical left can't do, how we need both to listen.

I watch someone's PET scans and can't get the colours
out of my head, they glow fuschia, violet, raspberry.
Each orange idea bathes the inside of my skull
with a sodium light show of patterns and predictions.
I think of wet molecules sliding themselves

from one warm dark place to another,
and a good idea as a surfeit of electrons.

Thinking in music, it seems, is natural to us,
hardwired for intervals and expectations,
programmed to the crackle of synaptic events, heartbeats,
breathing, the smooth imperatives of machinery.

But I can't explain from what I know, the blind savant,
unable to tie his shoelaces at 21, only just learned
to make a cup of tea, who plays the piano like the water
of the whole of his life is flowing through him.
He plays while the others talk, drowns them out.
When he stops he rocks. Backwards. Forwards.

That night – a room full of metronomes out by a fraction,
the whole thing periodically coming together
then swinging apart in a mad disintegration,
the small aberration that changes everything.

Listen then, to the music,
to the surge of your blood and its backwash.
The welling and subsidy of pain is like the passing
of a train, which the savant plays as a dissonant chord,
shifts to another and he has it perfectly as it hurtles off
into the night, or a train which didn't pass but stayed
with him and became part of what he carries everyday,
every waking the start of another journey, like it or not,
and all the way to the end of the line,
that chord underneath.

3.   Light coming down the stairwell,
the house quiet and a sense of no easy way out.
A spider tries to climb out of the bath,
keeps going at the same old thing
and dropping back, getting no further.

I come up against the same old God,
same old stairs to the sky, same old
mirror and my colossal reflection.
If there is a way out it's not here.

I go with the sparrow outside who is singing
there is no God there is no God there is no God.

4. What there is, is the future, going on somehow.
It glides up to us, a gilded fish with scales
of silk and bronze, waving its filaments and spines,
the gills rose red and complex as a city.
Its tight mouth is talking bubbles
but knowing the names of all the molecules
in the sea doesn't translate the message for us.

5. Half a mile away over the fields, the Methodists
belt out songs to Jesus at a wattage that's hyperbole.
He's a long way up so they have to shout
and I don't know whether to laugh or cry
because it didn't used to bother me, live and let live,
even, once upon a time, I envied their certainty
but they were at it till midnight and I was awake
and fretting about the world getting stuck on Retro,
going fundamental all over again, how we should
know better. That and Jehovah's Witnesses
buying the old village hall, asbestos and all.

So much for mass, time and light!
So much for addressing what's numinous
directly, full on, as much as we can bear it,
coming out from behind the pillars of the past
and being small but standing there, our chance
to blow the trumpet loud and clear, to swig back
the wine and butter the bread, to realise
that grace is in the biology of man.

As for all those ladders up to the sky –
forests of them, because we needed them way back
when life was so terrible all we could think of
was something better somewhere else –

those ladders; we must chop them down for firewood
and the mirror, we must smash it to smithereens,
so that looking up, we see the sky as space-time
and learn to deal with that, see what difference it makes.

III

Waves

Glen Brittle

On the south west side of the island –
our campsite, the empty beach, no birds.
Landward, black peaks edging to the sea
and sheet lightning up among the crags.
That way is remote. I'd never get there.
Briefly, the sun is a terrible light.

A stream runs off Sgurr Alasdair
all the way down, then reaches the edge
of the moor and an easy drop
onto rock onto rock onto rock
then clearing the final fall
is water mixing with sky
till I can't tell but something is shining
as it's broken to bits in the sea.

It's hard to look. A channel of crazy water.
All the quarrels of the sea swilling in
and back till the water's all temper.
I edge to the rim of the land
considering what's barely begun.
Could I push someone? Could I ever
jump if need be, to escape, say,
or to save a man? I'm dumb.

Nothing in the world would carry me into that.
So where can I go from here
where the road stops,
and all the mountains can't be climbed
and the sky has a terrible light
and the open sea is what's ahead?

Tender to Miss Judith

She's high and dry on marsh grass
along with *The Nipper*, *Sea Spray* and ducks
and the North Sea is nowhere in sight,
an idea held in trust. This could be Kinder
with boats on, if it weren't for Barnacle geese
sticking their necks out above the reeds,

if it weren't for oystercatchers chirruping,
redshanks mating, that open, that free.
We're breathing deep when from out there
comes a weather of Brent geese. Thousands.
Thousands of them shaping and reshaping
at the farthest reach of our glasses.

A passing lifeboat man asks what we're looking at,
says he wouldn't walk half a mile out there,
not for a thousand pounds, not for two
he's that scared of water. Needs to know
where he stands, needs a boat,
something solid between him and it.

Waves

Because they all seemed to be enjoying themselves,
the boys from the cafe riding the surf with trays,
and because you so much wanted me to try,
I followed you out. When you said
What on earth is there to be afraid of here?
I couldn't name it

but knew it was that first hint
of the long pull out even at knee-deep,
sucking at the floor, at my feet.
It was about the physiology of the sea,
how it crashes back, the same wave
dragging its long weight always.

It was about when to jump, or whether,
then being thumped off balance
and knowing myself underwater but not which way up,
hoping that force of personality or patience would do
till I could breathe but not knowing how long
and please God needing the wave to drop now.

It was my backside hitting bottom
then kicking hard and my head pushing up
through foam with the shame of panic
salting my eyes, fierce at the back of my throat.

It was turning around
and the next one already coming.

In the Lifeboat

We cry like babies, ten of us, trying to stay afloat. Another man tries
to swim to us but a great sea from the north sweeps him out of sight.
The captain dies, then one dies every hour. If I don't give up,
not by one small inch, might that be the thing to save me?

On the morning of the fourth day or the fifth the dawn comes clean,
the sea calms, even the sun. Three left. It cannot end like this.
For them, but not for me. Something will turn up and the wind
and the cold and the troughing sea will be only fright remembered.

Look at them. One is lolling. The stomach of the other is frozen.
But it's me who's lolling head back on the wooden side
with the sea slopping at our bottom boards, shifting its depths
where I daren't look, only at the horizon. Will a foreign ship come?

We have no clothes. The sea goes up and down. On the morning
of the seventh day, him and me. The sea is silver. And the sun.
Whatever's before or after, those who drown, simply drown.
Our boat is a small boat going up and down.

Under the Icecap

When blood slows
in the chambers of his idling heart

and his peripheral vessels shut down,
does he notice the chill? Is he afraid?

One tungsten light. Rotate it slowly. Back
across blue-green subtleties and gaps

so black they might pass straight down
to everlasting cold. This is zero.

He is careful along passages
of Prussian blues and greens. Nothing

is biological. There is no life
to obscure things. It is quite clear.

Expect dark, expect salt, expect ice,
he told himself, but he did not know.

In this climate, nothing
has ever replaced itself

except the thin intent of the ice
building the cold muscle of the sea.

Sediment

We duck beneath the surface and slip into half light,
leaving fish circles, as we sink to the sea bed
to the great blue-glazed moraines
that are shadowed as a range of hills might be.

We touch down on sand. Soft. White. A rare light
traps the alkaline colours of Parrot fish nibbling on coral.
A Lizard fish swallows something whole.
Damselfish dart for safety to the coral's inner folds.

I'm almost upon a Blue Spotted Lagoon ray
half buried in the sand. He plunges off.
Silver fish flicker in and out the eyes of a human
skull that's settled into stones and shells.

A single intact femur's close beside, nothing else.
What might have been has metamorphosed to coral fans
with alizarin fronds, to the creature colours of violet,
viridian and crimson lake. Beyond that the floor drops.

We venture far enough to see what's trailing fangs,
then sea slugs, the undulating mottled skins
of flat amorphous things and others with no heads
or heads with buds instead of eyes. And the precipice.

Beyond that, the bottomless deep, its silence
a slow darkness where the only direction
would be our own bubbles moving upwards
and where nothing could stop us falling.

The Great White

Listen boy,
imagine the *Baby Ronald* out from Cape Town,
its bilge pumps broken down, three hundred foot of line
going straight to the bottom. The fin circles, goes below.

You could tell
it was a Great White. When we got him out you saw
his lower teeth, the gum, an eye looking at you till you'd swear
he knew. Older than the dinosaurs, that one.

I told him,
Die. Die, you bastard but he wouldn't.
Harpooned through the gills six times, gushing blood –
an apex predator, his will programmed in –

eyes rolling
and that obscene threshing. Five times the revolver
and the relief of it done. I took the fin
but couldn't put the hook back in the ocean.

At the end of the day,
we towed him and two hundred others
on a five kilometre line astern, clouds of bubbles
milking the sea and the sky breaking up all rosy.

Tough shit boy,
and you with the smell of the city still on your flesh,
I've got to live. Him or me is what it comes down to.
There's only so much life to go round.

Rescue

My father is swimming straight out towards a waving hand and a shout for help. At the water's edge, his wife is holding onto his jacket and the hand of their small daughter.

This is the sea he grew up with, the cold, washing-up water sea. He is a good swimmer so why is halfway so much further than he thought? ... *a woman is swimming beside him* ... Out there the hand again and the hand not ... *close to, the woman swimming* ... and the swell's immediate horizon. Then the hand not. No hand anywhere on the too-late sea ...

... then he has him, the boy's face alive or dead with no way to tell but at least he has him which just makes it worth the long way back ... *the woman close beside him every inch of the way* ... Later, 'Beautiful' my father said 'like an angel.'

My mother's always told me how an ambulance took the boy alive or dead, about my father's trousers stripped clean off him by the sea with all their holiday money in the pocket, how they'd gone home and stopped at a police station to ask about the boy without saying why, that my father had a week in bed and never spoke of it again.

My mother found the poem in his pocket, about the woman in the sea and didn't like to say anything because he didn't. She kept it for years then burned it out of respect when he died and now regrets that, really wishes she hadn't.

So do I. I'd know it by heart, something to hang on to, a way to reach out and come close to my father as he swims on his own in the empty sea.

Snorkelling

Finally I let go your hand and was floating face down
by myself in the precious sea. When I looked,
a net of light was veined across the underwater sand.
Everything else was light-headed turquoise
and there were small striped fish that didn't bother me.
Shoreward it was all sand and shallows and two
white ducks, upended. I could have laughed
but the other way, the darkening colour was everything
I didn't know about the Libyan Sea.

You said *Come out further* and I hardly dare
but you promised not too far and dived between my legs
counting ten of the little stripey fish who liked so much
of what we were stirring up around my ankles.

I could hardly believe the nakedness of one foot, yours,
and my own hands underwater were suddenly beautiful
I thought, and your body kept pace, absolutely clear,
absolutely certain. Even your nails, I was that close,
became pink shells and your bubbles where you broke
the lid of the sea were small spheres of exhaled light.
I followed your body further into the ancient and modern sea,
wide-eyed in filtered light, sometimes looking seaward
then shoreward quickly, but mainly sticking close,
dealing with the immediate and my otherwordly hands.

Floating, Face Down

The sea always makes me want to love you more.
I do want to, believe me, but we're waist deep already
and I behave as if the whole ocean were below
and quite beyond me. I can't judge depth in water
and dare not turn my back on the sea for an instant.

Face down, floating's just about okay, in fact
nothing to it, this being wet and moved. Forget fish
(you'd said about the bigger fish over by the rocks
and how you'd like to get me there), forget them,
light is what catches me, the veining on the sea bed,
cobbles shape-sliding, my hands and feet larger
than life and the all-importance of breathing.

I face a free shadow of myself, my own edges
are building, unbuilding in a web of fluent light
that travels from me, running before what must be a breeze,
with the floor sliding faster and faster and then the shock
when I lift my head to check and find I'm facing out to sea,
not even out of my depth but farther than I thought
and just looking that way is enough to see how
it could happen if only I were brave or foolish
enough to pursue it, the light running along the floor
and the urge to go with it, to keep on streaming.

Holiday Ocean

From the quay:

light on a white hull, a watery aurora
spreading sheets of light on the paintwork.
A fisherman dunks a tea bag and rocks the boat.
The light goes berserk, recovers, reverses,
citrine shreddings from the sun fish-scaling the entire side;

the water is sequined herringbone
and there's a tapping stay on other boats
I could've been sailing in around the margins of the world
and a sea I could go swimming in the shallows of
with the other people who've come here,
the ocean risen by the exact presence of our bodies,
each molecule making a difference;

a ferry off-loads passengers and takes on
fresh crowds immediately, there's the siren
of it leaving on a ghostly rose sea, with the sun
going down on the other side of the island.
Bow wave and wake reach the shore together,
coming in as bigger waves, turbulence, choppy interferences.

I fix a point near my feet and stare at its dissolution
to dark and light and dark again but can't keep track
of it, not even one point on the surface of the sea,
which is how it has to be in a chaotic system,
you just have to let it happen, like the broken crests
and currents and moving troughs of other people's lives
going on by themselves, each with its own imperative.

All I can do is watch.

Chania, Old Town

From the lighthouse;

three colours banded,
aquamarine, turquoise, lapis further out.

Venetians and Arabs came here,
built the minaret at the harbour tip
which cuts the tide wide open.
Inside; the lagoon, the harbour cafes.

                    *

We focus right down
thinking how colour only comes with depth
and how even shallow water changes
these grains of sand, those vacillating stones,

also, that if we study for long enough
their granulations, their sedimentary colours,
this is our best chance to learn
what stones know about the sea.

                    *

Not so long since gold
was traded weight for weight with salt,
the Arabs taking tons of it from the Sahara,

fourteen hundred camels once recorded
leaving Tamchekt, headed south,
the Bantus that eager for the sea on their lips.

                    *

In the goldsmith's street:

> turquoise, brilliants, Russian bands,
> dolphins, lapis lazuli square set
> in old Cretan rings.

> We are precious gravels,
> we are lustre, inclusions, silk
> and indulgent Pharaoh gold.

We focus sapphires through a lens
and are face down in brimming ultramarine,
ducking under the venous sea and sluicing up into love,
a place to come home to. So the sea runs

and I might hope to be the colour of that sea,
that the sea might take me from the land
till the land is out of sight and I'm open
to absolutes, resolving always to the elements
of turquoise, lapis and ultramarine.

Diana Syder is a freelance therapist, lecturer and writer. She lives in the Peak District.

Hubble won The Poetry Business Competition 1996.

For details of Smith/Doorstop publications, *The North* magazine, our monthly Writing Days and the current Book and Pamphlet Competition, contact:

The Poetry Business, The Studio, Byram Arcade, Westgate, Huddersfield HD1 1ND